D0251573

A
Story Told
a Child

Christmas
Every Day

By William Dean Howells
Foreword by
Richard Paul Evans

POCKET
BOOKS

POCKET BOOKS, a division of Simon & Schuster Inc.
1230 Avenue of the Americas, New York, NY 10020

Foreword copyright © 1996 by Richard Paul Evans

ISBN: 0-671-00326-7

First Pocket Books hardcover printing November 1996

10 9 8 7 6 5 4 3 2 1

POCKET and colophon are registered trademarks of Simon & Schuster Inc.

Printed in the U.S.A.

Christmas Every Day was first published in 1908.

Interior design and illustrations by Gina DiMarco
Interior artwork by John Lawrence

*S*hortly after my book *The Christmas Box* was published, I began receiving calls from readers asking where they could find a copy of William Dean Howells's *Christmas Every Day*, the book Richard reads to his little girl in *The Christmas Box*. I soon realized how fortunate I had been in "stumbling" across the tale as I learned that it had not been in print since 1908.

I had come across the tale accidentally. As I assembled the pieces of my own Christmas tale, I decided that I needed more interaction between the father, Richard, and his daughter, Jenna. Nothing seemed more natural than the father reading a story to his young daughter—a Christmas story. Rummaging through boxes of ornaments, decorations, and Christmas books, I came across a volume of short holiday stories. Inside was William Dean Howells's *Christmas Every Day*. I was unfamiliar with the story but not with its writer. At the turn of the century, Howells was one of America's most influential men of letters. He was outspoken, intellectual, a champion and close friend of many of the most controversial writers of the day, including Mark Twain and Henry James. Why did Howells write a children's story? And a Christmas story at that?

As I read the first paragraph, I couldn't believe my good fortune to have discovered such treasure—a story about a young girl asking her busy father to read to her. As I went on to read the whole story, I embraced its simplicity and charm and decided to use it in my book. It would be several years after the writing of *The Christmas Box* that, to my astonishment, I would discover just how relevant Howells's story really was to mine.

Howells, the proud father of three children, saw exceptional promise in his youngest daughter, Winifred. "Winifred," Howells doted, carried herself with "angelic dignity" for "every impulse in her was wise and good." In a letter to his father, Howells related how, during the holiday season, Winifred would come to him in the parlor, where Howells would pretend to descend the chimney and then bestow Christmas gifts to his beloved child, certainly reminiscent of *Christmas Every Day*.

As Winifred grew, so did his admiration for the young girl, prompting him to write, "I would say she is in every way my equal, but I would fear that should be an insult to her."

In 1889 Howells's life was to change forever. Winifred, at the young age of 25, took ill and died.

Howells was inconsolable. Like MaryAnne in *The Christmas Box*, Howells stretched himself out on his daughter's grave and, as he later wrote to a friend, "experienced what anguish a man can live through." His bereavement "left life in a shadow not to be lifted on earth." He wrote to the novelist Henry James, "I wonder how we live. It seems monstrous." Then later he wrote that he had "tired of living and longed to be with *her*."

Though he desperately felt the desire to write about his daughter, he felt incapable of producing a worthy tribute. *Christmas Every Day* is a rare exception. Written three years after her death, *Christmas Every Day* is not as much about Christmas as it is about a father's love for his daughter. And in this I found still greater connection, for *The Christmas Box* was written not for the world, but for my two little girls, Jenna and Allyson.

Even more surprising, to me, than that he would leave the heady realm of social commentary to write a simple Christmas tale is that he would probe those locked recesses of his heart that most dare not enter in themselves lest they bring pain. And then, once inside, he drew not of his heart's angst but of its light and simple love. Perhaps this is what he meant when he wrote, "If there can be any comfort, it is that death cannot take away what she once was."

There is one more lesson to be learned from Howells's writing. If I had once held to the notion that in times past all children were more properly seen and not heard, it was subtly dispelled by this tale's loving and playful interaction between a father and his daughter. Then, as today, little girls wrapped their fathers around their fingers and held them tightly in their hearts—demonstrating to all of us that love between parents and children is not just timeless, but ageless.

It is a joy that, after nearly a century, *Christmas Every Day* is again brought to print. This is a story to be embraced for its warmth and wisdom—and truly there is wisdom in all Christmas storytellers. For as long as there are Christmas stories, there will be fathers and mothers sharing them with children. And in matters of Christmas there is nothing so magical as a parent's love.

With love and Christmas,
Richard Paul Evans

Christmas Every Day

he little girl came into her papa's study, as she always did Saturday morning before breakfast, and asked for a story. He tried to beg off that morning, for he was very busy, but she would not let him. So he began:

"Well, once there was a little pig—"

She put her hand over his mouth and stopped him at the word. She said she had heard little pig-stories till she was perfectly sick of them.

"Well, what kind of story *shall* I tell, then?"

"About Christmas. It's getting to be the season. It's past Thanksgiving already."

"It seems to me," her papa argued, "that I've told as often about Christmas as I have about little pigs."

"No difference! Christmas is more interesting."

"Well!" Her papa roused himself from his writing by a great effort. "Well, then, I'll tell you about the little girl that wanted it Christmas every day in the year. How would you like that?"

"First-rate!" said the little girl; and she nestled into comfortable shape in his lap, ready for listening.

"Very well, then, this little pig— Oh, what are you pounding me for?"

"Because you said little pig instead of little girl."

"I should like to know what's the difference between a little pig and a little girl that wanted it Christmas every day!"

"Papa," said the little girl, warningly, "if you don't go on I'll give it to you!" And at this her papa darted off like lightning, and began to tell the story as fast as he could.

ell, once there was a little girl who liked Christmas so much that she wanted it to be Christmas every day in the year; and as soon as Thanksgiving was over she began to send postal-cards to the old Christmas

Fairy to ask if she mightn't have it. But the old Fairy never answered any of the postals; and after a while the little girl found out that the Fairy was pretty particular, and wouldn't notice anything but letters——not even correspondence cards in envelopes; but real letters on sheets of paper, and sealed outside with a monogram——or your initial, anyway. So, then, she began to send her letters; and in about three weeks——or just about the day before Christmas, it was——she got a letter from the Fairy, saying she might have it Christmas every day for a year, and then they would see about having it longer.

The little girl was a good deal excited already, preparing for the old-fashioned, once-a-year Christmas that was coming the next day, and perhaps the Fairy's promise didn't make such an impression on her as it would have made at some other time. She just resolved to keep it to herself, and surprise everybody with it as it kept coming true; and then it slipped out of her mind altogether.

She had a splendid Christmas. She

went to bed early, Christmas Eve, so as to let Santa Claus have a chance at the stockings, and in the morning she was up the first of anybody and went and felt them, and found hers all lumpy with packages of candy, and oranges and grapes, and pocket-books and rubber balls, and all kinds of small presents, and her big brother's with nothing but the tongs in them, and her young lady sister's with a new silk umbrella, and her papa's and mamma's with potatoes and pieces of coal wrapped up in tissue-paper, just as they always had every Christmas. Then she waited around till the rest of the family were up, and she was the first to burst into the library, when the doors were opened, and looked at the large presents laid out on the library-table—books, and portfolios, and boxes of stationery, and breastpins, and dolls, and little stoves, and dozens of handkerchiefs, and inkstands, and skates, and snow-shovels, and photograph-frames, and little easels, and boxes of water-colors, and Turkish paste, and nougat, and candied cherries, and dolls' houses, and waterproofs—and the big Christmastree, lighted and standing in a wastebasket in the middle.

She had a splendid Christmas all day. She ate so much candy that she did not want any breakfast; and the whole forenoon the presents kept pouring in that the expressman had not had time to deliver the night before; and she went round giving the presents she had got for other people, and came home and ate turkey and cranberry for dinner, and plum-pudding and nuts and raisins and oranges and more candy, and then went out and coasted, and

came in with a stomach-ache, crying;
and her papa said he would see if his
house was turned into that sort of fool's
paradise another year; and they had a
light supper, and pretty early everybody went to bed cross.

Here the little girl pounded her
papa in the back, again.

"Well, what now? Did I say pigs?"

"You made them *act* like pigs."

"Well, didn't they?"

"No matter; you oughtn't to put it
into a story."

"Very well, then, I'll take it all out."

So the father went on:

he little girl slept very heavily, and she slept very late, but she was wakened at last by the other children dancing round her bed with their stockings full of presents in their hands.

"What is it?" said the little girl, and she rubbed her eyes and tried to rise up in bed.

"Christmas! Christmas! Christmas!" they all shouted, and waved their stockings.

"No such thing! It was Christmas yesterday."

Her brothers and sisters just laughed.

"We don't know about that. It's

Christmas to-day, anyway. You come into the library and see."

Then all at once it flashed on the little girl that the Fairy was keeping her promise, and her year of Christmas was beginning. She was dreadfully sleepy, but she sprang up like a lark—a lark that had over-eaten itself and gone to bed cross—and darted into the library. There it was again! Books, and portfolios, and boxes of stationery, and breastpins—

"You needn't go over it all, papa; I guess I can remember just what was there," said the little girl.

Well, and there was the Christmas-tree blazing away, and the family picking out their presents, but looking pretty sleepy, and her father perfectly puzzled, and her mother ready to cry. "I'm sure I don't see how I'm to dispose of all these things," said her mother, and her father said it seemed to him they had had something just like it the day before, but he supposed he must have dreamed it. This struck the little girl as the best kind of a joke; and so she ate so much candy she didn't want any breakfast, and went round carrying presents, and had turkey and cranberry for dinner, and then went out and coasted, and came in with a—

"Papa!"
"Well, what now?"
"What did you promise, you forgetful thing?"
"Oh! Oh yes!"

Well, the next day, it was just the same thing over again, but everybody

getting crosser; and at the end of a
week's time so many people had lost
their tempers that you could pick up
lost tempers anywhere; they perfectly
strewed the ground. Even when people
tried to recover their tempers they usu-
ally got somebody else's, and it made
the most dreadful mix.

The little girl began to get fright-
ened, keeping the secret all to herself;
she wanted to tell her mother, but she
didn't dare to; and she was ashamed to
ask the Fairy to take back her gift, it
seemed ungrateful and ill-bred, and
she thought she would try to stand it,

but she hardly knew how she could, for a whole year. So it went on and on, and it was Christmas on St. Valentine's Day and Washington's Birthday, just the same as any day, and it didn't skip even the First of April, though everything was counterfeit that day, and that was some *little* relief.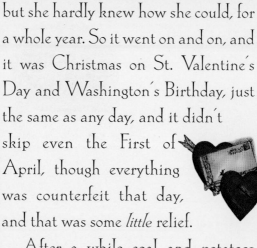

After a while coal and potatoes began to be awfully scarce, so many had been wrapped up in tissue-paper to fool papas and mammas with. Turkeys got to be a thousand dollars apiece—

"Papa!"

"Well, what?"

"You're begin-
ning to fib."

"Well, *two* thou-
sand, then."

$And they got to passing off almost
anything for turkeys—half-grown
hummingbirds, and even rocs out of
the *Arabian Nights*—the real turkeys
were so scarce. And cranberries—
well, they asked a diamond apiece for
cranberries. All the woods and
orchards were cut down for

Christmas-trees, and where the woods and orchards used to be it looked just like a stubble-field, with the stumps. After a

while they had to make Christmas-
trees out of rags, and stuff them with
bran, like old-fashioned dolls; but
there were plenty of rags, because people got so poor, buying presents for one
another, that they couldn't get any new
clothes, and they just wore their old
ones to tatters. They got so poor that
everybody had to go to the poor-house,
except the confectioners, and the fancy-
store keepers, and the picture-book
sellers, and the expressmen; and *they* all
got so rich and proud that they would
hardly wait upon a person when he
came to buy. It was perfectly shameful!

Well, after it had gone on for about three or four months, the little girl, whenever she came into the room in the morning, and saw those great, ugly, lumpy stockings dangling at the fireplace, and the disgusting presents around everywhere, used to just sit down and burst out crying. In six months she was perfectly exhausted; she couldn't even cry any more; she just lay on the lounge and rolled her eyes and panted. About the beginning of October she took to sitting down on dolls wherever she found them— French dolls, or any kind—she hated the sight of them so; and by Thanksgiving she was crazy, and just slammed her presents across the room.

By that time people didn't carry presents around nicely any more. They flung them over the fence, or through the window, or anything; and, instead of running their tongues out and taking great pains to write "For dear Papa," or "Mamma," or "Brother," or "Sister," or "Susie," or "Sammie," or "Billie," or "Bobbie," or "Jimmie," or "Jennie," or whoever it was, and troubling to get the spelling right, and then signing their names, and "Xmas, 18——," they used to write in the gift-books, "Take it, you horrid old thing!" and then go and bang it against the front door. Nearly everybody had built barns to hold their presents, but pretty soon the barns overflowed, and then they used to let them lie out in the rain, or anywhere. Sometimes the police used to come and tell them to shovel their presents off the sidewalk, or they would arrest them.

"I thought you said everyone had gone to the poor-house," the little girl interrupted.

"They did go at first," her papa said, "but after a while the poor-house got so full that they had to send the people back to their own houses. They tried to cry, when they got back, but they couldn't make the least sound."

"Why couldn't they?"

"Because they had lost their voices, saying 'Merry Christmas' so much. Did I tell you how it was on the Fourth of July?"

"No; how was it?" And the little girl nestled closer, in expectation of something uncommon.

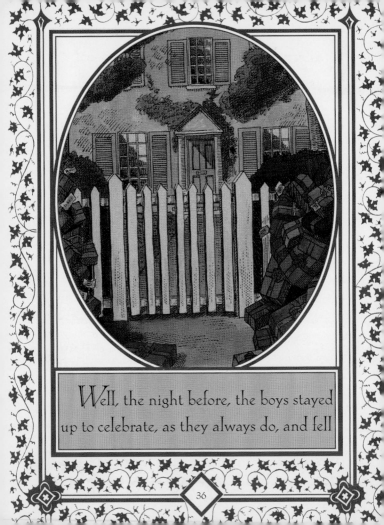

Well, the night before, the boys stayed
up to celebrate, as they always do, and fell

asleep before twelve o'clock, as usual, expecting to be wakened by the bells and cannon. But it was nearly eight o'clock before the first boy in the United States woke up, and then he found out what the trouble was. As soon as he could get his clothes on he ran out of the house and smashed a big cannon-torpedo down on the pavement; but it didn't make any more noise than a damp wad of paper; and after he tried about twenty or thirty more, he began to pick them up and look at them. Every single torpedo was a big raisin! Then he just streaked it

upstairs, and examined his fire-crack-
ers and toy-pistol and two-dollar col-
lection of fireworks, and found that
they were nothing but sugar and candy
painted up to look like fireworks!
Before ten o'clock every boy in the
United States found out that his
Fourth of July things had turned into
Christmas things; and then they just
sat down and cried—they were so
mad. There are about twenty million
boys in the United States, and so you
can imagine what a noise they made.
Some men got together before night,
with a little powder that hadn't turned

into purple sugar yet, and they said they would fire off *one* cannon, anyway. But the cannon burst into a thousand pieces, for it was nothing but rock-candy, and some of the men nearly got killed. The Fourth of July orations all turned into Christmas carols, and when anybody tried to read the Declaration of Independence, instead of saying, "When in the course of human events it becomes necessary," he was sure to sing, "God rest you, merry gentlemen." It was perfectly awful.

The little girl drew a deep sigh of satisfaction.

"And how was it at Thanksgiving?"

Her papa hesitated. "Well, I'm almost afraid to tell you. I'm afraid you'll think it's wicked."

"Well, tell, anyway," said the little girl.

Well, before it came Thanksgiving it had leaked out who had caused all these Christmases. The little girl had suffered so much that she had talked about it in her sleep; and after that hardly anybody would play with her. People just perfectly despised her, because if it had not been for her greediness it wouldn't have happened; and now when it came Thanksgiving, and she wanted them to go to church, and have squash-pie and turkey, and show their gratitude, they said that all the turkeys had been eaten up for her old Christmas dinners, and if she would stop the Christmases, they would see about the gratitude. Wasn't it dreadful? And the very next day the little girl began to send letters to the Christmas Fairy, and then telegrams, to stop it. But it didn't do any good; and then she got to calling at the Fairy's house, but the girl that came to the door always said, "Not at home," or "Engaged," or "At dinner," or something like that; and so it went on till it came to the old once-a-year Christmas Eve. The little girl fell asleep, and when she woke up in the morning—

"She found it was all nothing but a dream," the little girl suggested.

"No, indeed!" said her papa. "It was all every bit true!"

"Well, what *did* she find out, then?"

"Why, that it wasn't Christmas at last, and wasn't ever going to be, any more. Now it's time for breakfast."

The little girl held her papa fast around the neck.

"You sha'n't go if you're going to leave it so!"

"How do you want it left?"

"Christmas once a year."

"All right," said her papa; and he went on again.

ell, there was the greatest rejoicing
all over the country, and it extend-
ed clear up into Canada. The people met
together everywhere, and kissed and cried

for joy. The city carts went around and gathered up all the candy and raisins and nuts, and dumped them into the river; and it made the fish perfectly sick; and the whole United States, as far out as Alaska, was one blaze of bonfires, where the children were burning up their gift-books and presents of all kinds. They had the greatest *time!*

The little girl went to thank the old Fairy because she had stopped its being Christmas, and she said she hoped she would keep her promise and see that Christmas never, never came again.

Then the Fairy frowned, and asked her if she was sure she knew what she meant; and the little girl asked her, Why not? and the old Fairy said that now she was behaving just as greedily as ever, and she'd better look out. This made the little girl think it all over carefully again, and she said she would be willing to have it Christmas about once in a thousand years; and then she said a hundred, and then she said ten, and at last she got down to one. Then the Fairy said that was the good old way that had pleased people ever since Christmas began, and she was agreed.

Then the little girl said, "What're your shoes made of?" And the Fairy said, "Leather." And the little girl said, "Bargain's done forever," and skipped off, and hippity-hopped the whole way home, she was so glad.

"How will that do?" asked the papa.

"First-rate!" said the little girl; but she hated to have the story stop, and was rather sober. However, her mamma put her head in at the door and asked her papa:

"Are you never coming to breakfast? What have you been telling that child?"

"Oh, just a moral tale."

The little girl caught him around the neck again.

"We know! Don't you tell *what*, papa! Don't you tell *what*!"